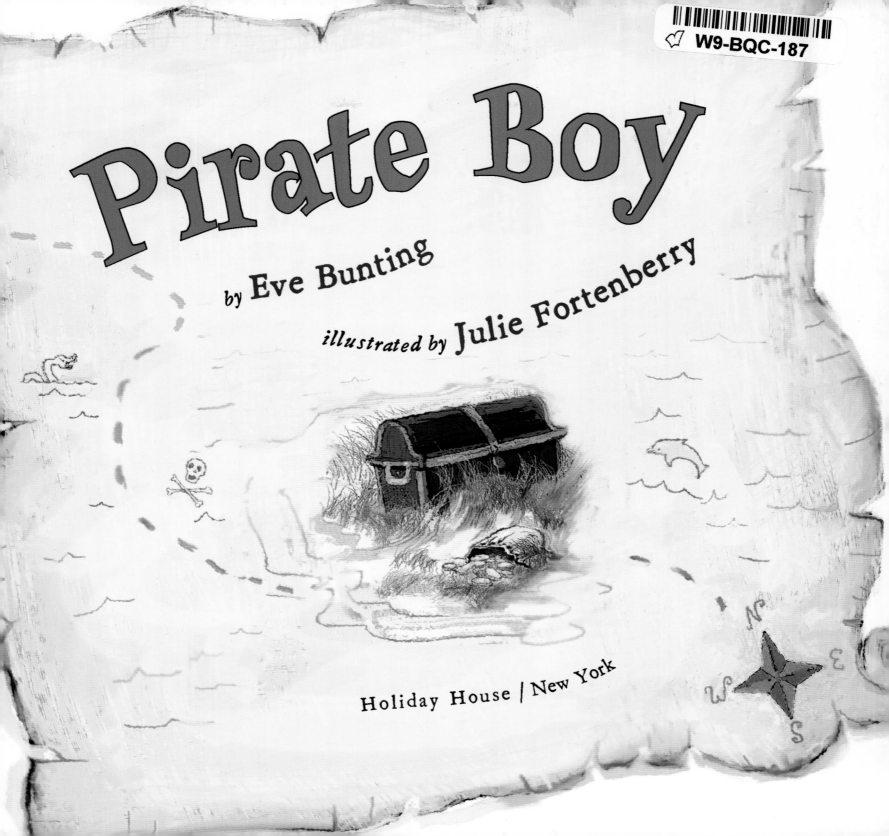

Pirate Boy

by **Eve Bunting**

illustrated by **Julie Fortenberry**

Holiday House / New York

W9-BQC-187

Text copyright © 2011 by Eve Bunting

Illustrations copyright © 2011 by Julie Fortenberry

All Rights Reserved

HOLIDAY HOUSE is registered in the U.S. Patent and Trademark Office.

Printed and Bound in December 2015 at Toppan Leefung, DongGuan City, China.

The text typeface is Grit Primer.

The artwork was painted digitally using Adobe Photoshop.

www.holidayhouse.com

5 7 9 10 8 6 4

Library of Congress Cataloging-in-Publication Data

Bunting, Eve, 1928-

Pirate boy / by Eve Bunting ; illustrated by Julie Fortenberry. — 1st ed.

p. cm.

ISBN 978-0-8234-2321-7 (hardcover)

[1. Mother and child—Fiction. 2. Pirates—Fiction.

3. Imagination—Fiction.]

I. Fortenberry, Julie, 1956– ill. II. Title.

PZ7.B91527Phj 2011

[E]—dc22

2010029446

ISBN 978-0-8234-2546-4 (paperback)

To Keelin Bunting, our pirate girl
—E. B.

For John
—J. F.

Danny and his mom were reading a book called *Pirate Boy*.

When they came to the end, Danny said, "Mom? What if I want to be a pirate and sail away on a pirate ship?"

"Then I will be sad," Mom said.

"But, Mom?" Danny asked. "What if I don't like it on the pirate ship? And I want to come back home?"

"Then I will ask a nice, friendly dolphin to take me out to that pirate ship, and we will bring you home."

"Okay. But, Mom, what if you can't find a nice, friendly dolphin?"

"I will find one. But if I can't, I will swim out to the pirate ship."

"Okay. But, Mom, what if there are sea monsters, and they want to eat you up?"

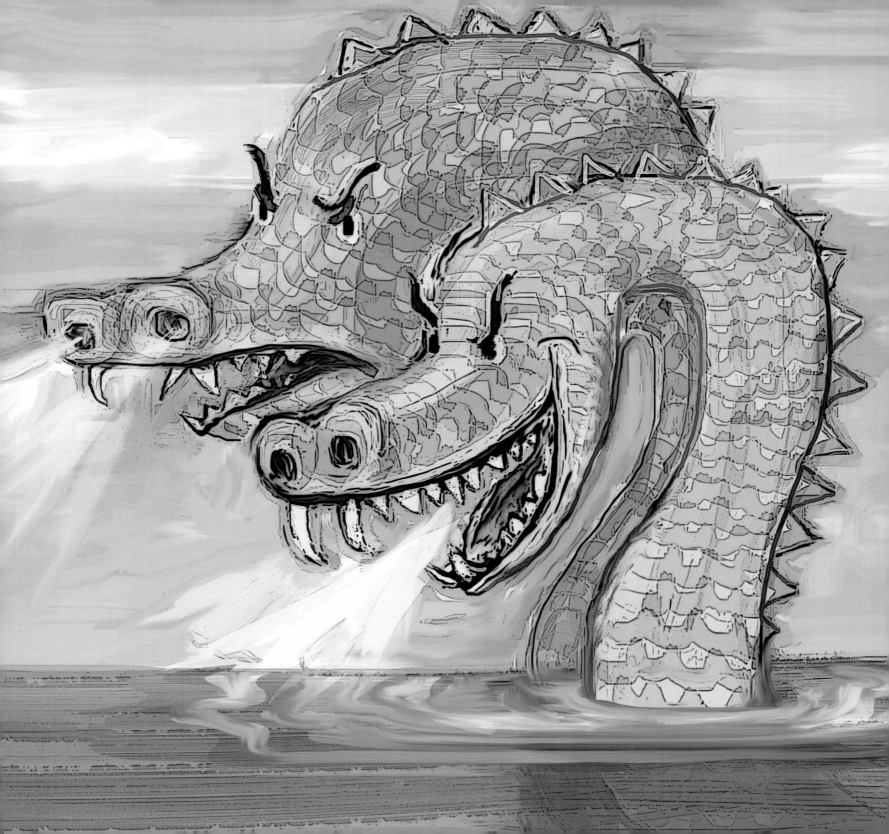

"Then I will spray them with my magic spray.
SSSSSSS. And they will get smaller and smaller and smaller.
They will be as small as your goldfish."

"Okay. But, Mom, what if you get to the pirate ship, and the pirates like me and don't want me to go?"

"I will tell them that you are my little boy and I am taking you," Mom said.

"Okay. But, Mom, what if
they're bigger than you?"

"I will spray them with my magic spray, and they will get smaller and smaller and smaller. *SSSSSSS.* They will be no bigger than bugs."

"Okay. But, Mom, I didn't know you had a magic spray. Can I see it?"

"I do have a magic spray," Mom said. "I cooked it up today and put it in this spray bottle. So we will be ready."

"Okay. But, Mom, after you spray the pirates and they're small, small, small and they can't hurt us, how will we get home?"

"I think the dolphin will be waiting for us. But if he isn't, you and I will take over the pirate ship, and we will sail it to Summer Beach."

"My best beach! And can I be the pirate captain?"

"Aye, aye, Captain."

"And then what will we do?"

"We'll leave the pirate ship on the beach, and we'll run all the way home."

"Okay. But, Mom, what will happen to the pirates? Now they are as small as bugs, and they won't be able to sail their pirate ship. And they were not really bad pirates."

"I will leave the magic spray. They can spray themselves big again and sail away."

"Okay. And, Mom, can we play on Summer Beach before we run all the way home?"

"Absolutely," Mom said. "We'll find shells and sea pebbles and make a sand castle. Then we'll go home."

"Okay. Will Daddy be there?"

"He will."

"And can I be the one to tell him about the pirates and the sea monsters and the magic spray, and about being captain of the ship?"

"You can."

"And we'll all have cookies and milk?"

"I don't see why not."

"And, Mom, I'm going to give you the biggest cookie on the plate because you are the bravest mom in the whole world. Okay?

"And, Mom, if I decide to go to the moon and I don't like it there, will you come and get me?"

"I will."

"Okay, Mom. Here's your cookie."